Special thanks to Valerie Wilding

ORCHARD BOOKS

First published in Great Britain in 2016 by The Watts Publishing Group

1 3 5 7 9 10 8 6 4 2

Text copyright © Working Partners Ltd 2016
Illustrations copyright © Working Partners Ltd 2016
Series created by Working Partners Ltd

A CIP catalogue record for this book is available from the British Library.

ISBN 978 1 40834 115 5

Printed in Great Britain

MIX
Paper from
responsible sources
FSC® C104740

The paper and board used in this book are made from wood from responsible sources

Orchard Books
An imprint of Hachette Children's Group
Part of The Watts Publishing Group Limited
Carmelite House, 50 Victoria Embankment, London EC4Y 0DZ

An Hachette UK Company
www.hachette.co.uk
www.hachettechildrens.co.uk

Katie Prettywhiskers to the Rescue

Daisy Meadows

ORCHARD

To Friendship Forest

Shimmer Lake

Beach

Snow
Swimmi

Pier

Map of Sapphire Isle

Bubbling Brook

Bucket and Spade Shop

Prettywhiskers' Purrfect Ice Cream Parlour

Admiral Greatwing's House

Shimmer Lake

To Grizelda's Tower

Can you keep a secret? I thought you could!

Then I'll tell you about an enchanted wood.

It lies through the door in the old oak tree,

Let's go there now - just follow me!

We'll find adventure that never ends,

And meet the Magic Animal Friends!

Love,
Goldie the Cat

Contents

CHAPTER ONE

A Magical Boat Ride

Crisp autumn leaves crunched beneath Lily Hart's boots as she tossed a spadeful of soil into a wheelbarrow.

She and her best friend, Jess Forester, were helping Lily's parents to dig a new pond near the Helping Paw Wildlife Hospital. Mr and Mrs Hart ran the

hospital in a barn in their garden, and
both girls loved caring for the animals.
Jess's dad, Mr Forester, was helping
too. As the five of them dug, they were
watched curiously by the animal patients
sitting in the nearby pens. Bunny noses
woffled, a chicken clucked and a fox
cub's ears twitched.

"This pond's much bigger than the old
one was!" said Jess.

"It needs to be," said Mrs Hart. "We
have so many ducks at the hospital now."

"And it's not just ducks who'll love the
new pond," said Mr Hart. "Frogs and

toads will come and use it too."

"And newts and dragonflies," added
Mr Forester. "It'll be like an animal
village!"

Lily and Jess shared a smile. The
girls knew they were both thinking the
same thing – that the pond sounded
like Friendship Forest! The forest was a

magical world where the animals talked, and lived in little cottages and dens. It was the girls' special secret.

After a little while, Lily's dad wiped his forehead and leaned on his spade. "Shall we go inside and have a cup of tea?"

"Good idea," said Mr Forester.

"Jess and I will put the tools away first," offered Lily.

The three grown-ups went into the house and the girls stowed the spades in the tool shed.

Jess sighed as she closed the door after them. "I wonder when Goldie will come

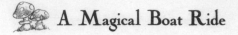

to get us again," she said.

Goldie the cat was their magical friend

who took them to Friendship Forest.

"I hope it's soon," said Lily.

Then Jess gave a start.

Something fluffy was

rubbing the back

of her legs!

Jess looked

down and laughed

in delight. A

beautiful golden

cat was standing

beside them.

"Goldie!" cried Jess. "This means we're going to the forest right now!"

With a mew, Goldie turned towards Brightley Stream, at the bottom of the garden.

Excitement tingled through Lily and Jess as they followed her. They knew time would stand still while they were away, so their parents wouldn't worry that they'd gone. Goldie led them towards an old dead tree in the middle of a meadow.

The girls ran after her, their hearts racing. They knew what was going to happen next!

Magically, the
tree burst into life.
Orange and gold leaves
opened, as dazzling as the autumn
sunshine. A flock of chattering starlings
swooped down to nibble the berries
hanging from every twig.

Jess and Lily stooped
to read the two words
written in the tree's bark.
"Friendship Forest!" the
two of them said together.
Immediately, a door with a
leaf-shaped handle appeared

in the trunk. Jess opened it, letting shimmering golden light spill out.

Fizzing with excitement, Lily and Jess stepped inside. They felt the tingle that meant they were shrinking, just a little.

As the light faded, the girls found themselves in a sunlit woodland glade. Their scarves and wellies had disappeared, replaced with jeans and light, fluttery T-shirts. The trees glowed crimson and yellow, while conkers and acorns dotted the forest floor. Flowers and berries nodded on bushes, and wonderful scents wafted on the gentle breeze.

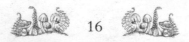

And there was Goldie, standing upright, wearing her glittery scarf.

"Welcome back," she said happily.

The girls hugged her.

"I'm so glad you're here," said Goldie. "I want to take you somewhere you've never been before!"

"Wow!" said Jess. "Where's that?"

But Goldie just smiled. "Wait and see," she said mysteriously.

The excited girls followed her through the forest.

As they walked,

their friend Mr Cleverfeather, the owl,
flew overhead. As well as his waistcoat
and monocle, he wore a sailor's hat.
"Nice bay for the deech!" he called as he
few past, muddling his words as usual.

Jess looked at Lily. "What did he say?"

"I think he meant, 'Nice day for the
beach'!" Goldie giggled. "Come on!" she
said. "We're nearly at Shimmer Lake."

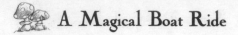

Moments later, they reached the shore
of of a beautiful, gleaming lake. Huge
lily pads bobbed towards them. A frog
stood on each one, holding a long pole.

"It's the Greenhops!" Jess cried.
"Hello!"

"Hop, hop, hop aboard!" said Mr
Greenhop.

"But where are we going?" asked Jess, as she stepped onto a lily pad.

"You'll see in a moment," said Goldie, her green eyes shining.

The Greenhops pushed off with their poles and the lily pads bobbed over the crystal-clear lake. Then, through the hazy sun, the girls saw a lush green island.

"Wow!" gasped Lily.

"That's where we're going," said Goldie. "To Sapphire Isle!"

CHAPTER TWO

Purrfect Ice Cream

"It's beautiful!" said Jess, as the lily pad got closer to the island. Sandy beaches glistened in the sunshine and trees swayed in the gentle breeze.

There were lots of boats on the lake. Some had sails, some had oars, and there was even a barge captained by a

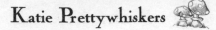

duck in a red bow tie.

"It's the Featherbill family!" cried Lily, waving to little Ellie the duckling, who was jumping up and down on the deck.

Molly Twinkletail and her nine brothers and sisters paddled a long canoe, each wearing tiny yellow life jackets. The Fuzzybrush foxes were in a rowing boat, and the Scruffypup dog family sped past

 22

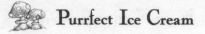

in a yacht with billowing sails.

"Everyone's going to Sapphire Isle," Goldie told them. "You'll see why when we get there."

When the lily pads reached a little wooden jetty, the girls jumped off.

"Thanks for a lovely ride!" said Lily.

"You're welcome," said Mr Greenhop. "Have a wonderful day!"

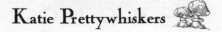

The girls looked around. Tumbling
streams and waterfalls sparkled in the
sunshine, and beyond was a hill, sprinkled
with orange and lemon trees. Pastel–
coloured cottages dotted the shore.

"It's so pretty!" said Lily.

Goldie led the girls along the edge of
the beach. To the girls' amazement, the
sand wasn't just yellow – it was a whole
rainbow of colours.

Sitting on the sand were lots of animals,
busy building sandcastles.

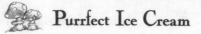

Goldie smiled. "It's the annual Sapphire Isle Sandcastle Competition!"

"That looks fun," said Lily, "especially with such lovely sand. Let's have a go!"

Goldie took the girls' hands in her paws. "I want to show you something else first – the best ice cream in Friendship Forest!"

They went to a pale pink building at the top of the beach with little tables and chairs outside. The sign above the door said: "Prettywhiskers' Purrfect Ice Cream Parlour".

Before they reached the door, a little ginger tabby kitten with bright green eyes rushed out to meet them. She wore a sun visor with a strawberry embroidered on it.

"You're Jess and Lily!" she said, clapping her paws in delight. "My cousin Bella Tabbypaw told me about you two. I'm Katie Prettywhiskers!"

"Hello, Katie," said Lily.

"We'd love to try some of your ice cream," said Jess with a grin.

Katie grinned back. "Come in," she said. "I bet I've got the *purrrrfect* flavour for you."

There were more tables inside. Great

Uncle Greybear waved from where he was eating a big bowl of pink ice cream, drizzled over with toffee sauce. On the counter there were big tubs, each filled with a different coloured ice cream, and a table piled with cones, bowls of sprinkles and jugs of sauce.

"Mmmm," sighed Jess, breathing in the sweet, creamy smells. "This is amazing!"

Katie led them into a room at the back. "This is where we make the ice cream," she explained.

Shelves were filled with boxes of nuts, chocolate, raspberries and all kinds of

28

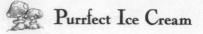

other ingredients. In the middle of the room was a huge ice cream maker. It had a wooden wheel, a funnel on top and a bowl underneath.

"It's like the Dreamy Creamy Ice Cream Machine that Mr Cleverfeather gave Goldie for her birthday," said Lily, "but much bigger!"

"He made this one, too," Katie said. She looked closely at Goldie for a moment. "I know just what flavour you'd like…"

Then the kitten darted around the room, pulling boxes from the shelves and spooning ingredients into the funnel.

Finally, she poured in a jugful of ice

crystals and turned the wheel.

The machine began to whir.

Moments later, pink ice cream swirled

into the bowl. Katie scooped it into a

cone and gave it to Goldie. She gave it a

lick.

"Wow!" cried

Goldie. "Strawberry

hazelnut – that's

my favourite

flavour! How

did you

know?"

Katie grinned. "I just do! Why don't you go and sit down, and I'll bring Jess and Lily's favourite flavours, too."

"But you don't know what our favourites are," said Jess.

The kitten's bright eyes twinkled. "Let me guess."

Mrs Prettywhiskers, Katie's mum, came in wearing an apron. She showed the girls and Goldie to a table. A few moments later Katie appeared, carrying two ice cream cones.

Lily tasted hers. "Mint chocolate chip – my favourite! And it's so delicious!"

"Mine's cherry," said Jess. "That's *my* favourite. How did you know, Katie?"

Mrs Prettywhiskers tickled the kitten's ear. "Guessing favourite flavours is Katie's special talent," she said. "We don't know how she does it!"

Jess's eye was caught by something on a shelf high above the cones and sauces. It was a beautiful blue shell.

"That's so pretty!" she said.

"It is," agreed Katie, "and there's something very precious inside it!"

She climbed onto a chair, took something out of the shell and held it

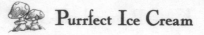

out to the girls and
Goldie.

It was a brilliant
blue star-shaped
gem.

"It's one of the
four sapphires that
protect the island,"
said Katie. "A
different family
looks after
each one, and
each has a different
power. Ours keeps the

water of the Shimmer Lake at the perfect temperature."

"Wow," said Lily, gazing at the sapphire. It flashed and sparkled in the sunlight streaming through the window.

"The shell keeps the sapphire safe," Katie told them. "As long as it's in the shell, no one can harm it."

Before she could put the sapphire back, they heard a shout from outside the ice cream parlour.

"There must be trouble at the beach!" cried Goldie. The girls and Goldie put their cones in the bin and ran outside.

 34

The animals on the beach had stopped
making their sandcastles. They were
watching a huge grey ship, covered in
slimy seaweed, that was approaching
Sapphire Isle. A tattered flag, showing a

cauldron and crossed brooms, flew from
a tall pole. Dirty yellow sparks shot from
the ship's funnel, which let out a blast, like
the sound of a hundred rusty trumpets.

Standing at the ship's wheel, steering
it towards the shore, was a tall woman
in skinny trousers and pointy-toed black
boots. Her cloak billowed over her purple
tunic and her green hair whipped behind
her.

"Oh, no," cried Jess. "It's Grizelda!"

CHAPTER THREE
The Water Imps

Jess and Lily looked at each other worriedly. Grizelda the witch was always coming up with nasty plans to make the animals leave Friendship Forest, so she could have it all to herself! The frightened animals scattered to hide behind rocks or sandcastles.

 37

The ship stopped by the jetty. "Well, well, well," Grizelda sneered. "It's the meddling girls and the interfering cat. You won't stop my plan this time!"

"Go away, Grizelda!" Goldie told her. "Leave the island in peace!"

Grizelda cackled. "No chance, cat. I'm going to steal a sapphire!"

The girls heard horrified gasps from the animals, cowering in their hiding places.

Grizelda laughed. "Ha! Without the sapphires' protection, the lake will be ruined and the animals will have to leave the island. Then it'll be mine!"

Jess stepped forwards. "Why are
you doing this? Sapphire Isle is no use
to you!"

Grizelda scowled. "It is!" she shrieked.
"I'll name it Sorcery Isle, and I'll build a
holiday tower by the beach."

"We'll stop you!" Lily told her.

"You won't," Grizelda sneered. "My
new servants will make sure of it."

Four tiny creatures sprang out from
behind Grizelda and landed on the jetty.

"Meet my water imps," said Grizelda.

The imps stood as tall as the girls'
ankles. They had blue skin and wore

39

hats, tattered trousers and stripy tops.
One of them carried a net made from
seaweed. "Ahoy there, land lubbers!"
he cried.

"That's Kelp," said Grizelda.

"They're like little pirates," Lily
whispered to Jess. "Kelp's even got a
wooden leg!"

The second imp had a gold earring on one ear. She patted her tummy. "Ain't it lunchtime yet?" she asked. "I could eat a whole pondweed cake!"

"She's called Urchin," said Grizelda.

The third imp, who wore a belt with a shiny buckle, had clambered up the side of a rock and was hanging on with

just one hand. "Ahoy there," she said. "I be Barnacle."

Grizelda pointed to the fourth imp. "And that's Shrimp."

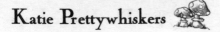

He was smaller than the others and wore yellow armbands. "This be a fine island for plundering treasure!" he said.

"They don't look like they can do much harm," Lily said doubtfully. "They're so tiny."

But Jess wasn't listening. She'd spotted Katie and Mrs Prettywhiskers hurrying along the beach towards them. Something was glittering in Katie's paws.

"Oh, no!" she cried. "Katie's still holding the sapphire!"

"Katie!" Goldie yelled. "Put the sapphire back! Grizelda wants to—"

It was too late. Grizelda had spotted the sapphire and began to chant:

"Sapphire vanish from this place!
Disappear and leave no trace.

Where you hide,
the imps will know.
My spell will tell
you where to GO!"

As she spoke
the last word,
she pointed a
bony finger,
sending yellow
sparks shooting

towards the sapphire.

In a flash of light, it vanished.

Katie stood still, her face frozen in
dismay.

The girls were horrified.

"Grizelda, give that back!" Jess yelled.

"No! And you'll never find it," the
witch cackled nastily. "My water imps
will make sure of that." She turned to
them. "Go!"

"We'll guard the sapphire, me hearty,"
said Kelp. "We love treasure!"

The imps ran away so quickly that
they were four small blurs. Sand sprayed

up into the air as they smashed the
sandcastles in their path.

Grizelda gave a final cackle and spun
the ship's wheel. Smelly sparks spat
from the funnel as she sailed away from
Sapphire Isle.

Katie was in tears. "This
is all my fault!" she
sobbed. "I shouldn't
have brought the
sapphire out here!"
Lily cuddled
her, stroking
the kitten's soft

fur. "Please don't cry! We'll get it back." She turned to Jess. "I wonder what will happen now it's gone?"

"It's already happening," Jess replied grimly. "Look!"

Ice was creeping over the lake. As the girls watched in horror, waves turned to ice and boats that had been bobbing on the water were frozen in place. The ice swept over the sand too, freezing the sandcastles.

"Run," cried Goldie, "before it freezes all of us, too!"

Goldie, the girls and all the animals

46

hurried off the beach, just in time to see ice forming over the ice cream parlour.

Jess pulled Lily and Goldie aside. "We must get that sapphire back into its shell," she said. "Or Sapphire Isle will be frozen for ever!"

CHAPTER FOUR

Admiral Greatwing's Map

Lily looked out at the frozen lake. She could see animals shivering in the boats that were stuck in the ice. "Poor things," she said. "They'll never be able to go home unless we fix this. But where do we start?"

 49

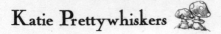

"If the imps are guarding the sapphire," Jess said, "we need to find out where they went. Let's ask if anyone saw."

"Good idea," said Goldie. She turned to the Fuzzybrush foxes, who were huddled by one of the pastel-coloured houses. "Did you see where the imps went?" she asked.

The foxes all shook their heads. "They shot away too quickly," said Mr Fuzzybrush.

The girls and Goldie went across the ice to where the Featherbills' barge was frozen into the lake. They were flapping their wings, trying to keep warm.

"Did you see where those imps ran off to?" Lily asked.

"We've no idea," Mrs Featherbill replied. "They disappeared so fast. What a flapdoodle!"

They asked lots of other animals, but nobody could think where the imps might be. Goldie and the girls went sadly back to Katie and her mum.

"I know who could help!" Mrs Prettywhiskers said. "Admiral Greatwing the albatross. He's an old sailor with lots of maps. One of them is a magical map that shows where the sapphires are."

"Brilliant!" said Lily. "Where does the admiral live?"

"I know the way!" said Katie. "Can I go, Mum? I want to help!"

"All right, then," agreed Mrs Prettywhiskers. "But be careful!"

Katie led the girls and Goldie along a wide path into the middle of the island. Even though they were

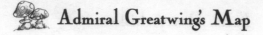

moving away from the ice, it was cold.

Katie shivered, her whiskers trembling.

They reached the foot of a hill and

looked up to see an astonishing sight:

a boat on top of the hill, its sails

flapping in the breeze!

"How did it get up

there?" wondered Lily.

"Surely it can't have been

shipwrecked!"

Katie led them up the hill. When they got closer, they saw that the boat had a front door.

"It's a little house!" said Jess.

"Ahoy there!" called a booming voice.

They looked up at a crow's nest made from a tall pole with a big barrel on top. Sitting inside it was a huge bird wearing a sailor's hat decorated with gold braid. He had a white head and neck, and sharp black eyes. Tucked beneath one dark wing was a telescope.

Katie cupped her paws around her

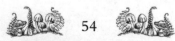

mouth. "Admiral Greatwing, can you help us? It's really important!"

The albatross put down the telescope and stretched his enormous wings. "Look out below!" he boomed. Then he leaped out of the crow's nest and glided to the ground.

"Wow!" Jess whispered. "His wings are wider than my bedroom!"

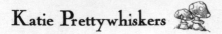

"What's wrong, Katie?" the admiral asked. His voice was even louder now he was next to them.

"Our sapphire's been stolen," she replied, "so the lake and the beach have frozen over! It's awful!"

"By my feathers!" exclaimed the admiral. "What a terrible tale. Come inside and tell me more."

Goldie and the girls followed Katie and the admiral into the boat. While Katie explained about Grizelda and the imps, Jess and Lily looked around.

Rolled-up maps were stacked

 56

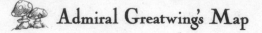

everywhere: on shelves, in vases, under chairs, even in the spout of an old teapot. Models of sailing ships stood on a huge chest. On a table was a large bowl of blue-green berries and a huge jug of cream.

"So you see," finished Katie, "we really need your map so we can get the sapphire back. Please can we borrow it?"

"Of course!" Admiral Greatwing pointed one of his huge wings towards the table. "Seaberries and cream always set me up for a long voyage. Help yourselves to some while I find the map."

Lily and Jess realised how hungry they
were when Goldie served them all bowls
of blue-green fruit and thick cream.

"Mmm, these are yummy," said Jess, as
she ate one of the seaberries. It tasted like
a mixture of apple and raspberries.

"I should make seaberry ice cream,"
said Katie, licking cream from her paw.

Admiral Greatwing was rummaging in

 58

a wooden chest. "Here it is!" he boomed.

He spread a map on the table. It was made of soft sea-green paper, and apart from place names, the only things marked on it were four blue shapes. There was a star, a droplet, a flower and a heart.

"The shapes show where the sapphires are," the admiral explained. "If the sapphires move, the shapes move, too."

"That's amazing!" said Lily.

Katie looked closely at the map. "Our sapphire's star-shaped," she said. "It looks like it's at a place called Bubbling Brook."

Jess jumped up. "Let's go!"

"Take the map with you," said Admiral Greatwing. He opened a cupboard and pulled out four woolly jumpers in different sizes. "Take these, too. It's chilly out there, thanks to that ice."

"Thanks, Admiral," they replied, putting the jumpers on.

"Purrrrfect!" said Katie, snuggling into her tiny one.

Admiral Greatwing showed them to the door. "Good luck, brave voyagers!" he boomed, as they set off. "I hope you find that sapphire!"

CHAPTER FIVE

After Those Imps!

The four friends followed the map to the centre of Sapphire Isle. They clambered to the top of a rocky hill, looking down at a sparkling pool. The fronds of a weeping willow tree almost touched the water. Huge bubbles the size of beach balls were floating around on the

 61

surface, glistening with rainbow colours in the sunshine.

"That must be Bubbling Brook!" said Katie, who was holding the map. "The sapphire's down there somewhere."

"Ssh!" whispered Lily. "Someone's there."

Four little figures threw their hats into a heap and leaped into the pool.

"The water imps!" said Goldie.

Jess watched Kelp, Urchin and

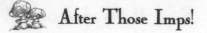

Barnacle dive, roll and swim. "They're amazing swimmers," she said.

"All except Shrimp," said Katie.

The smallest imp stayed near the shore, shrieking with laughter as he splashed about.

Goldie said thoughtfully, "They're having so much fun that we might be able to climb down and look for the sapphire without them noticing. We can stay out of sight behind that willow tree."

They crept down the hillside as quietly as they could. When they got closer, they could hear the imps talking as they swam.

"Yo-ho-ho!" cried Kelp gleefully, as he burst one of the big floating bubbles. "Grizelda will be as pleased as a parrot that we've stopped anyone from finding the sapphire!"

Urchin swam into another bubble, popping it. "Then she'll give us the reward she promised – a ship of our own!"

"So that's why the imps are helping Grizelda," Lily said.

The four friends moved silently around the pool, keeping hidden behind the willow branches. They'd only gone a few steps when Jess caught her breath. Something was glittering inside one of the bubbles floating in the pool.

"The sapphire!" she whispered. She reached towards the bubble, trying to burst it, but the bubble floated past.

"I'll try," said Goldie. She darted along the bank and stretched out for the bubble, but it floated past her, too.

Lily picked up a stick from the ground and ran past Goldie. She leaned towards

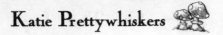

the bubble, gently sweeping it towards

the shore with the stick. When it was

close enough, Lily grabbed at the

sapphire. Her hand popped the bubble

and it burst, covering her in rainbow-

coloured spray. Lily was so surprised that

she toppled into the pool.

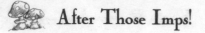

SPLASH!

Lily sat up, spitting out water. But in her hand was the sapphire!

"Brilliant!" whispered Jess, grabbing Lily's other hand and pulling her from the water. "Now, let's go before the imps notice us!"

But the imps had stopped playing.

"What be that noise?" Urchin wondered out loud.

"There!" screeched Barnacle, pointing to Lily and Jess. "They've looted the sapphire! After them!"

Kelp, Urchin and Barnacle swam

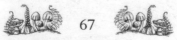

towards Jess and Lily quickly. Shrimp
splashed along behind them.

"Water bombs!" cried Urchin. She
pulled parcels made from seaweed from
her pockets and flung them at Goldie and
Katie. The cats shrieked as the bombs
burst, soaking them.

Then Urchin
lobbed
another at
Lily. It exploded
on her shoulder,
showering her
in water.

As she shook water from her eyes, Kelp leaped up with his net – and caught the sapphire from her hand.

"Yo-ho-ho!" cried Kelp in delight. "We got our loot back, me hearties!"

The imps cheered and zoomed off, disappearing up the hillside.

"I can't believe it," Jess groaned.

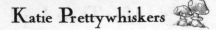

"We've lost the sapphire! And we're soaked!"

"I know," said Lily with a sigh. Then she glanced down. "That's funny – my clothes are dry!"

"Mine, too!" said Jess.

"I'm not wet at all," said Goldie, checking her tail.

"It must be thanks to Admiral Greatwing's jumpers!" said Katie. "I think they're magical!"

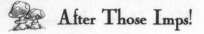

They clambered back up the rocky
hillside and Katie unrolled the map. The
sapphire was moving back towards the
beach, and they hurried after it.

As they got closer to the frozen lake,
the air became colder. The cottages and
shops were frosted white, and when they
reached the shore they had to be careful
not to slip on the icy sand.

Katie looked at the map again.

"Look," she said, "the sapphire's stopped here on the beach somewhere."

They looked around. There were the sandcastles, all iced over, but apart from some slimy seaweed from Grizelda's ship, there was nothing else. No imps. No animals. No one.

And definitely no sapphire.

CHAPTER SIX

Inside the Sandcastle

Katie's ears twitched in confusion as she looked around the deserted beach. "But where's the sapphire?"

"Maybe the imps buried it," suggested Goldie.

Jess dug her heel into the sand, but it was frozen solid – she couldn't even make

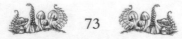

a dent. "I don't think they could," she said.

"Then there's only one place it could be," said Lily. "They must have hidden it inside a sandcastle."

Goldie crouched down beside the nearest sandcastle and tried to knock it over with her paws. "It's no good," she said, shaking her head. "It's frozen solid."

Katie tried to wriggle inside the doorway of another sandcastle, but she was too big. "We'd have to shrink to go inside any of these. But we can't do that."

Jess's face lit up. "We can!" she said. "With shrinking violets! Remember,

 74

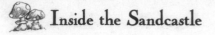

Goldie? We used some on our adventure with Amelia Sparklepaw."

"That's a great idea," said Goldie, "but shrinking violets grow by the Butterfly Bower, in the forest. We'd have to cross the frozen lake to fetch them. We can't ask the butterflies to bring some, because it's too cold for them."

Katie clapped her paws with excitement. "I know who can fly in cold weather!" she said. "Follow me!"

She led them, slipping and sliding, to a shop that sold buckets and spades, a little way from the beach. In a room at the back, an elderly seagull, wearing a pair of fluffy slippers, was reading to two youngsters.

"Hello, Katie," she said. "I heard about the sapphire. How terrible!"

"Hello, Grandma Gail," said Katie. "We're doing our best to get it back."

"Hello!" said the girls.

"Hello-ello-ello," the young seagulls said together.

"This is Skye and Marina Saltybill," Katie said. Then she turned to the seagulls. "Would you help us by fetching some shrinking violets? It's very important to save the lake."

Marina flapped her wings, "Of course, if Grandma Gail says it's OK!"

The elderly seagull smiled. "Off you go! Some exercise will warm you up."

"Goody-goody-goody," squawked Skye and Marina.

Goldie explained where to find the shrinking violets and Skye and Marina took off, shouting, "Bye-bye-bye!"

The friends thanked Grandma Gail and returned to the beach. "It'll take ages to explore all the sandcastles when we're tiny," said Jess. "Let's see if we can work out which one the imps are hiding in."

They made their way along the beach, checking each sandcastle. Some

had window openings they could peep
through, and most had arched doorways.

Lily crouched down to peep into a
big castle with a square tower. "There's
nothing inside," she said, looking up.

Katie brushed sand off Lily's nose.
"You got too close," she giggled.

After a while, they'd checked nearly all
the sandcastles on the beach. Jess kneeled
down next to one of the last ones. It was
huge, with turrets and a moat. Shells
decorated the walls and there was even a
seaweed flag on top.

"Psst!" Jess beckoned to the others.

"Someone's singing," she said.

They listened closely. Voices sounded
from inside.

"Row, row, row the boat

All around the lake.

Look for treasure in the deep.

How much can you take?

LOTS!

  80

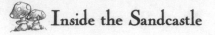

Row, row, row the boat,

Pile it high with gold.

Fill your pockets and your hat.

How much can you hold?

    LOTS!"

Lily grinned. "It's the imps!"

There was a cry from above the beach. "Hello-ello-ello!"

Skye and Marina Saltybeak swooped down and dropped a bunch of shrinking violets into Jess's hand.

Marina gave Lily some growberry blossoms. "You'll need these for getting back to your proper size," she said.

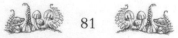 81

"Thanks!" said Lily, popping them in her pocket. "See you later."

"Good-luck-luck-luck!" squawked the seagulls, as they flew away.

Jess handed violets to Lily and Goldie, and found a tiny one for Katie. "You're so little already that we can't let you shrink too much," she said.

When they ate the flowers, Lily and Jess felt the same tingle they got when they stepped into the Friendship Tree, but for longer. They became smaller and smaller, until they were as tiny as the seashells dotted around the beach.

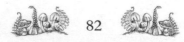

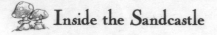

"Oh, wow!" said Jess. "Everything looks so different!"

They could see the shapes of different grains of sand, and tiny patterns on the shells. The ice covering the sand looked like a layer of diamonds.

"Look at the pebbles!" said Lily, gazing at one the same size as her, which had flecks of silver gleaming in it. "I never knew stones were so beautiful!"

Jess shivered. "It's even colder when you're small," she said. "Come on – let's go into the castle."

They tiptoed through the sandcastle

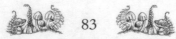 83

entrance and into a sandy
corridor. It was as beautiful inside
as it was outside, with gleaming
shells lining the walls and patterns
carved into the sandy floor.
Lily caught Jess's eye and the
girls grinned at each other. Even
though they were worried about
saving Sapphire Isle, they couldn't
help feeling amazed that they were
walking through
a sandcastle!

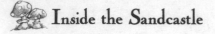

Ahead of them, Goldie rounded a corner, but quickly jumped back.

"It's the imps!" she said. "They're sitting around the sapphire eating seaweed."

The imps began another song.

"Seaweed! We love it.

Seaweed's so scrummy

In soup, buns and sarnies

Everything tastes yummy!"

They burped, then Urchin clapped her hands and said proudly, "We're never letting the sapphire out of our sight again, me hearties! Grizelda will soon be giving

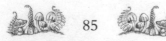

us a ship of our own. Then we can set

sail for all the adventures we can find!"

The four friends exchanged worried

looks and tiptoed out of the sandcastle.

When they were back on the icy beach,

Katie looked up at the girls with tear-

filled eyes. "How will we ever get the

sapphire back now?"

CHAPTER SEVEN

Katie's Purrfect Idea

Goldie, Jess, Lily and Katie sat outside the giant sandcastle, trying to work out what to do.

"That wasn't any help at all," sighed Jess. "We might as well eat the growberry blossoms."

She handed them round and they each

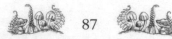

nibbled one. Lily and Jess felt a quivering
sensation as they grew back to normal.

"Going into the sandcastle *was*
helpful!" Katie cried. "That song the imps
were singing has given me an idea!"

"That's great!" said Lily. "What is it?"

"They were singing about how much
they like seaweed," Katie said. "I bet that's
their favourite ice cream flavour!"

"Yee-uck!" Jess and Lily said together.

Katie grinned. "I know, it must taste
horrible! But what if I made some, and
the imps came out to eat it? They said
they weren't letting the sapphire out of

 88

their sight, so they'd bring it out too."

"Great idea!" said Goldie.

"Wait," said Lily. "We can't make ice cream. The ice cream parlour is frozen."

Katie's whiskers drooped sadly. For a long moment no one said anything. Then Jess said, "Maybe we can't use the ice cream parlour, but that doesn't mean we can't make ice cream! We just need to use our imaginations. Admiral Greatwing had a huge jug of cream, remember? I bet he'd give it to us."

"Yes!" said Goldie. "We can ask Skye and Marina to fly and fetch some. Then

we can use ice from the lake to freeze it!"

Lily pointed at clumps of seaweed along the shore. "There's plenty to make it taste really seaweedy!"

Katie's eyes were shining. "This seaweed ice cream is going to be purrrfect!"

Not long afterwards, Katie was stirring all the ingredients inside a bucket. "It's working!" she purred happily.

The girls peered inside the bucket. It was filled with sludgy-green ice cream.

Lily sniffed, then wrinkled her nose.

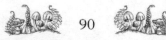

"Yuck," she said. "It stinks!"

Jess couldn't resist dipping in a finger and tasting it. "Urgh!" she said, with a shudder. "That's revolting!" Then she grinned. "I think the imps are going to love it."

Goldie carried the bucket to the sandcastle where the imps were hiding and left it outside. "They'll be able to

 91

smell it from here," she whispered.

Then the four friends hid behind a row of frozen deck chairs and waited.

They soon heard muttering voices, then Urchin burst out of the sandcastle.

"Shiver me timbers!" she shouted. "What be that scrummy smell?"

The girls held their breath. Would she like the ice cream?

Then Urchin ran towards the bucket and dived in, head first!

When her head poked up again, she was covered in ice cream. "Yummeeee!" she shrieked with delight.

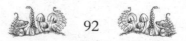

Barnacle ran out next, followed by Shrimp. They clambered into the bucket and scooped up handfuls of green ice cream, gobbling it greedily.

Finally, Kelp appeared – and he was clutching the sapphire!

"Gangway, mateys!" he yelled. "Let me at it!" He scurried towards the bucket. Just before he leaped into it, he tossed the sapphire onto the sand.

Jess crept out from behind the deck chairs. She

tiptoed towards the sapphire, glancing towards the imps to make sure they were still busy with the ice cream. *Just a few more steps and I'll be able to grab it,* she thought.

But then there was a shout.

"Girl ahoy!" yelled Barnacle.

Jess flung herself onto the hard sand, lunging for the sapphire. She grabbed it with both hands then rolled away from the imps.

She clambered to her feet and held the sapphire up. "Got it!" she cried.

CHAPTER EIGHT

Sandy Celebrations

"Shiver me timbers!" yelled Barnacle, as the girls raced away. "They've looted the sapphire!"

"Grizelda's going to be so angry! It's your fault, Kelp!" Urchin wailed.

"Is not!" Kelp replied. "You're the one who said there was ice cream!"

Jess, Lily, Goldie and Katie left the imps squabbling and hurried back to the ice cream parlour. Katie's mum was sitting outside, wrapped in a warm blanket.

Her eyes went wide when she saw what Jess was holding. "You've found the sapphire!" she cried. "I thought the island would be frozen for ever. Thank you so much, everyone!"

Lily grinned. "We couldn't have done it without Katie!"

"I'll tell you all about it later, Mum," said Katie. "We've got to get the sapphire back into its shell now, so its magic will

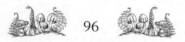

96

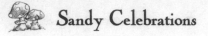

work – and so Grizelda can't steal it again!"

"I've got the shell right here," said Mrs Prettywhiskers. She held out the shell and Jess put the sapphire inside.

The blue gem glowed. Immediately, icy drops fell from the parlour roof.

"The ice is melting!" cried Lily.

They all hugged one another.

"We'll never take the sapphire out of its shell again," promised Katie.

They went outside and hurried down to the beach. Sand was already showing through the melting ice and boats were bobbing about in the water. When they ran to dip their hands and paws in the lake, the water was lovely and warm.

"It's purrrfect!" cried Katie.

There were happy shouts all along the beach as animals went running into the water, splashing and laughing. Admiral Greatwing flew in circles overhead.

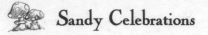

"By my feathers, you did it!" he boomed.

Lily smiled at her friends. "We did, didn't we? Sapphire Isle is safe again!"

Lily, Jess and Goldie were sitting on the warm sand with their friends, eating ice creams.

"And the winner of this year's sandcastle competition," said Grandma Gail, "is Admiral Greatwing!"

Everyone cheered. The admiral was standing by his sandcastle and raised one wing in salute.

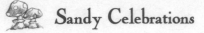

"Look!" cried Jess. "He made the sandcastle where the imps were hiding."

"He deserves to win," said Lily. "We know how amazing it is — both outside and inside!"

"The Prettywhiskers are kindly providing the prize," Grandma Gail continued. "A year's supply of ice cream in Admiral Greatwing's favourite flavour."

"Admiral, is your favourite seaberry with chocolate sprinkles?" called Katie.

"By my feathers, it is!" the admiral cried in amazement.

As the sun started to sink, Goldie, Lily and Jess said goodbye to their friends and climbed into Katie's boat. Katie took them back over Shimmer Lake to Friendship Forest. On the shore, they each hugged the little kitten goodbye.

"What a purrfect adventure," said Katie. "See you soon!"

They waved goodbye and made their way to the Friendship Tree. When they reached it, Goldie touched her paw to the trunk. A door opened, letting golden light shine out.

She hugged the girls. "I can't wait to

see you again."

"There are three more sapphires, aren't there?" asked Jess. "Come and get us if Grizelda tries to steal them, too."

"We're always ready to help Friendship Forest," added Lily.

Goldie smiled. "I know you are."

They stepped through the doorway.

When the light faded, the girls found themselves back in Brightley Meadow.

As they walked home, swishing their feet through autumn leaves, Jess said, "I know what everyone needs after all that pond digging. Ice cream sundaes!"

Lily grinned. "That sounds purrrfect!"

The End

A special boat race is taking place on Shimmer Lake. But Grizelda's horrible magic is turning the water dirty! Can little beaver Phoebe Paddlefoot help Lily and Jess bring back the sparkle?

Find out in the next adventure,

Phoebe Paddlefoot Makes a Splash

Turn over for a sneak peek . . .

The autumn sun was warm on Lily Hart's back as she fished a smooth, honey-coloured stone from Brightley Stream. She passed it to her best friend, Jess Forester, who put it in a basket.

"We've got loads of stones now," said Jess happily.

"Yes, we'll need another basket soon!" said Lily.

The stream was at the bottom of the Harts' garden, behind the Helping Paw Wildlife Hospital. Lily's parents ran the hospital in their big barn, and both girls loved to help care for all the poorly animals. They had helped their parents build a new pond there for the ducklings and goslings to enjoy as they got better. They hoped it would have plenty of visiting creatures, too — newts, frogs, toads, and even swans!

Jess stood on one of the stepping stones that crossed the stream. She peered into the crystal-clear water at grey stones with orange threads running through them. "Look at these," she said. "They'd make such a pretty border around the pond."

Lily jumped onto the stepping stone beside Jess to look. Then something jumped onto Lily's stepping stone!

It was a beautiful cat with a golden
coat and eyes the colour of fresh grass.

"Goldie!" Lily cried in delight.

The cat curled around her legs. Then
she did the same to Jess, before leaping to
the far bank and into Brightley Meadow.

"She's come to take us to Friendship
Forest!" cried Jess.

The forest was their special secret – a
magical world where animals lived in
little cottages and sipped blackberry tea
in the Toadstool Café. And, best of all,
they could talk!

Lily and Jess raced after Goldie towards a bare, lifeless tree in the middle of the meadow. The Friendship Tree!

As Goldie reached the tree, crisp yellow and crimson leaves sprang from the branches. A flock of squabbling jackdaws swooped down, and pink autumn crocuses dotted the grass below.

Read

Phoebe Paddlefoot Makes a Splash

to find out what happens next!

Jess and Lily's Animal Facts

Lily and Jess love lots of different animals –
both in Friendship Forest
and in the real world.

Here are their top facts about

CATS

like Katie Prettywhiskers :

- The first cats appeared on earth 3.6 million years ago.

- In Ancient Egypt, cats were worshipped as gods.

- Cats are very good at leaping, and they almost always land on their feet if they fall.

- A group of cats is called a 'glaring'.

Magic
Animal Friends

Can you keep the secret?

There's lots of fun for everyone at
www.magicanimalfriends.com

Play games and explore the secret world of
Friendship Forest, where animals can talk!

Join the
Magic Animal Friends Club!

✳ Special competitions ✳
✳ Exclusive content ✳
✳ All the latest Magic Animal Friends news! ✳

To join the Club, simply go to

www.magicanimalfriends.com/join-our-club/